Bad News on the Doorstep

an Arcadia Vyne Mystery

by

Ira Amos

James Kay Publishing

Tulsa, Oklahoma

BAD NEWS ON THE DOORSTEP
ISBN 978-1-943245-01-7

1.1

In Loving Memory of

I. A. & Kathleen Prestage

Special thanks is extended
to my wife
for her support and patience,
Jesse Whittle for his
artistic insight,
M. Carolyn Steele for her
always keen eye,
Mary Moore and
the wonderful staff of the
Tulsa City/County Library,
and finally,
a tip of the hat
to the late, great mystery author,
Rex Stout.

For He spoke, and it was done;
He commanded, and it stood fast.

Psalm 33:9 (NKJV)

The Players
in alphabetical order

Mr. George Arnold
(aka Tumbles)

Sergeant Griz Asher

Miss Phyllis Baxter

Baylee
(the chauffeur)

Officer Boggs

Pinky Bronson

Jake "Candyman" Caine

Mr. & Mrs. Chester

Mr. Jonas Cooper

Mr. & Mrs. Harmon

Mrs. Hidalgo

Jack
(the paperboy)

Mr. & Mrs. McCay

Mr. Jerry O'Dell

Miss Prunella Parks

Pug
(the diner owner)

Detective Burgess Raft

Rio Richards

Mr. Rodrick
(the secretary)

Miss Mary Smith
(the librarian)

Stewart
(the valet)

Mr. Arcadia Vyne

Tobias Watkins

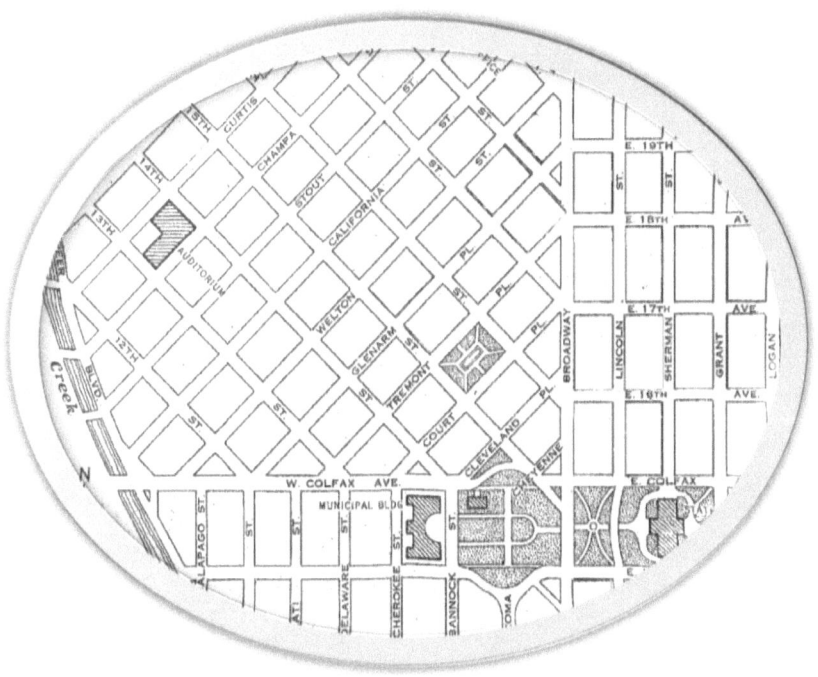

Denver, Colorado
Elev. 5280

ONE

On a list of sounds a person never wants to hear first thing in the morning, gunshots are right up there. Especially if it's a repetitive report announcing the arrival of two slugs of lead into the banister under your left hand. Tends to startle the right hand into spilling your coffee as it reaches for the bean shooter, which you forgot to put in the pocket of your bathrobe.

Options? Not numerous. Retreat? I'm more than halfway down. Stand still? I did mention I'm in Saturday morning attire, didn't I? Jump the rail? Of course. Why not?

So, I do and I land on top of, and slightly inside of,

the old folding hooded carriage Mrs. Hidalgo abandoned here last week. After untangling legs from cloth body and wire wheels, it's easy enough to duck for cover behind the damaged baby transport and reappraise the situation.

No more sounds emanate from beyond the doorway. Not the hot zing of bullets flying out of a gun at least. There's a creak from the third floor landing. Obviously the gal who lives above my cave is poking a nose out to satisfy her curiosity.

"Get back in your room!" I yell.

"What's going on down there?"

"Somebody is using the door for target practice. Go burn some toast and turn your Benny Goodman up real loud."

"You still sore about that?"

I was and I am. "Scoot!"

"Got a nickel? I'll call the cops."

"Left it in my other robe." What is her name? "Get back in your room!"

"Suit yourself." The door above slammed hard and immediately Benny's clarinet hit full volume, same as the three previous nights.

The apartment manager's door to my right cracked and tiny Mr. George Arnold (he once performed in the circus) ventured an eye and some of his own nose to investigate. "Jonas, you all right?"

"Fine, Tumbles, just fine. Don't come out."

It seems the retired clown didn't need to be told anything twice. He complied and slid the chain to keep the bad guys out.

My attention returned to the front door. A couple of holes allowed two dusty shafts of light access to the hardwood floor. My newspaper waited out there beyond those punctures and I wanted it. I didn't want a body lying on it. I didn't want blood on it. I did want to check the fight results of the Louis - Schmeling rematch. I did want to read the want ads. I did want to have coffee in my cup which would hold no more in this lifetime as pieces of it found their way to each of the steps I had decided to avoid on my way to this wonderfully safe and secure place behind the pram.

On most Saturday mornings since I'd taken residence in one of Denver's premier one star apartment buildings, I'd glide my way down the staircase in my most comfortable slippers, open the door, take my paper from the stack of three, glide my way back up to my room, and spend the rest of the day looking for work.

This particular weekend, the work may have come to me.

On the other side of the door.

Beyond the two bullet holes.

Meant for me?

I can sometimes be a bit arrogant, but I don't want to take all the credit.

Somebody else?

One way to find out. Coax my comfortable slippers to carry my tired feet over and open the door.

They did.

And there he lay.

Bad news on the doorstep.

Benny Goodman blared louder as the gal upstairs opened her door again and yelled down. "Hey! I'm expecting a delivery. If you see anybody with one, send him up."

"Sure thing."

"Thanks!" The door slammed and Benny hit a low note.

No delivery under the awning here. Just a pickup for the morgue. Five foot eight, nice shoes, better than a dime store suit, sandy flat-top, no hat. Overcoat no longer needed to fight the chill of this late June morning. He had a hole on the left side of his neck and the top of his corresponding ear was gone. But, why was he lying on his back with his legs heading up the steps? Left arm outstretched. Right hand up in the overcoat. He didn't croak in an instant ado, but he didn't crawl either. He should have at least slid down the face of the door, or if his knees buckled, fell forward onto his mug.

This didn't look right.

The neck wound was a through and through. Enough to smart for a while, and maybe enough to kill him. Absentmindedly I tried to turn the notched collar of my bathrobe up against the coolness of the morning.

I'd seen my share of stiffs back home, on the job. They'd call me first. "Find Cooper," they'd say. And I'd show and usually discover the guy had tried to pull a fast one on his boss, his sweetheart, his partner, his old lady, his bookie, or he'd been in the wrong place at the right time when one of the aforementioned went gunning for some other poor sap. Innocent bystanders are never innocent. There's always something else they're guilty of. Justice comes earlier for them than expected, that's all.

The guy lying here didn't look like any of those before. This chap looked surprised all right. A bullet will do that to you. But, he was twisted funny. Contorted like. Had somebody moved him between the time my coffee went all over my bathrobe until now? I'm thinking, yes.

Nobody on the street who didn't belong. Milkman,

a bus at the stop, shoeshine guy down in front of the Albany Hotel. The shiner didn't see anything. He can't see his own reflection in the toe of your Oxfords. Blind as the umpire at the Brooklyn Dodgers game I went to last summer when I was keeping an eye on what's-his-name. You know the guy. When I... Never mind. Let's not dig that horse up and run it again.

Okay, think about it. Nobody on the street who's not supposed to be.

Why not?

Man gets shot. Crowd forms. It's a given as night follows day. Where are all the gawkers? Sure, they're starting to get curious now. The scent of death travels fast. A few out of that building over there. Couple more poking eyes from the barber shop. One with a razor. One with shaving crème from ear to ear.

My curiosity moves from street inventory to body. Check it out before a local badge arrives.

I crouched and took a look-see. Perchance his wallet might be sticking out of his pocket enough to get a couple of fingers on it. No such luck. Nothing to get a vibe from. As average as the next Joe. Head tilted... Wait a second. There it is. He hit his head. That's why he succumb so fast. Not from the lead. From the fact some concrete reached out and wacked him one on the back of the noggin. Still, he should be up there. I studied the two steps to the door. Not down here among us and I refer to the aforementioned crowd now getting into the spirit of things.

"Who is he?" a lady with an apron up to her armpits asks.

"Never saw him before." Half shaved man.

"Ain't from 'round here." Scrawny barber.

"Young man, why are you out here half-clothed?" A grandmotherly type.

"Is he dead?" This one with a German accent.

"All right, all right. You in the pajamas. Step away, fella!" Denver's finest right behind my left ear. "Clear back, folks. Nothing to see. I'll take it from here. Nothing to see."

There was something to see. He didn't want them to be aware of it. But, I saw it. Somebody crowded the body a bit too close and bumped it with their shoe so the stiff's overcoat shifted. That's when I spotted it, but the cop put a meaty mitt on my shoulder and pulled me up by the cloth. This Joe was wearing handcuffs. One cuff secured around a broken wrist, the other secured around the handle of a briefcase. Problem. No briefcase secured to the handle.

The cop moved me back with his baton and took my former crouched position as his own. "This guy's been shot!" He stood and eyed the mob. "Okay, you lot. Stay put. One of our detectives is gonna want to talk to all of you."

That did it.

They scattered like crows in the face of a blast of buckshot.

"Hey, get back here!"

"I'm not going anywhere," I told him.

"Not you, fella. That lot. Get 'em all back here."

"Not my day to run the rodeo." This turned out to be a mistake.

My new cop friend, ten pounds heavier, about two inches taller, grabbed me by the ear and stuck his nightstick up into my throat. "Wise guy, huh? S'pose you tell me why you're out here this morning in last night's party clothes? An' what smells?"

"It's a bathrobe," I croaked, thinking if I cracked a few of his ribs for fun I might either spend a while in the clink or maybe share a slab next to Mr. Lucky sleeping at my feet. "Soaked in coffee."

"I know it's a bathrobe, you... Hey, where are you from, fella? Down south?"

"Oklahoma, I--"

"Yeah, I thought so." He twisted the stick. "You stand here real quiet like and wait for the detective. He's gonna want to talk to you."

I reached under the hem of my adversaries coat

and got my paw on his service revolver while his attention zeroed in on the blood draining from my face. Bad idea. For now. So, instead I pulled my hand back up to get hold of the stick.

"Gonna be smart again?" He leaned in nose-to-nose. "Fella."

"No, sir."

The stick retreated from my throat and I bent over to catch my breath. Remember when I said swiping his weapon seemed like a bad idea? Changed my mind and as I wheezed for air, I spirited it out of his holster, a trick I'd learned, among other forms of relieving someone from their possessions, from a pickpocket and snitch in my younger days. Like riding a bicycle, it went as planned and I flipped the rod behind me and into the gutter.

A patrolman appeared at the curb on a snazzy new Indian Scout. Two carburetors no less and polished to perfection. He was followed by a boxy, gangster-like black and white '37 Ford. A car fast as the wind in the home stretch, but difficult to stop when all was said and done. It braked as advertised with a squall and nudged its bumper into the rear tire of the Indian.

A stunted old man hiding behind thick glasses encased in black rims and wrapped in a layer of coats disembarked from the passenger side, walked behind the vehicle, cleared his throat, and tapped the beat cop on the shoulder. "Officer Boggs, pick your piece up out of the street." He pointed to the gutter, between the front and rear tires of the motorcycle, with a Chesterfield pipe he pulled from his pocket.

"Wha..." The young copper went for a quick draw and came back with air. "How'd..."

"Now, what have we got here, Sergeant Asher?" The old man adjusted his fedora by the crown, lit the pipe off a wooden match, and addressed his gorilla of a sidekick who had escaped from behind the wheel of the Ford. "Anybody ID this guy yet?"

I worked my way around behind them and leaned on a lamppost to observe.

Boggs, the cop with the short temper, threw a thumb over his shoulder at me. "Pajamas back there seems wise to the whole show."

"Name's not Pajamas," I shot back.

The old man turned and eyed me from under his hat. "Cooper, ain't it?"

He had me on that one and I didn't get how.

"Detective Raft. Burgess Raft." He closed the gap between us and offered a hand. "Saw you at headquarters when you came in to pick up your PI license. I don't forget faces."

"I'm impressed," I said because I was.

"You see who made this mug dead?"

"No."

"Why not?"

"I was busy dodging his secondhand slugs on the other side of that door." I pointed up the steps. "Two of the little darlins popped holes in the entrance and spilled my coffee as I descended the stairs."

The detective gave me the once over, memorizing every java stained thread of my robe. "You live here?"

"Where else?"

"You might be visiting a dame for the night."

"No. I'm on the second floor. Second door on the right."

"Who else lives here? This guy?" He pointed at our deceased visitor.

"Never saw him before."

I guess the grunt passed for an 'okay'. He just stared up at me and arched a brow over the rim of his glasses.

"Oh, my neighbors. You gonna write this down?"

"No."

"Suit yourself. Starting at the bottom, and working our way up, you've got the apartment manager, George Arnold--"

"Tumbles? This where he lives?" I think the detective may have smiled, but then again maybe not.

"That guy's a hoot. Who else?"

"Mrs. Hidalgo and baby Hidalgo, next to me on the left. A salesman on the right, never heard his name. He's on the road a lot."

"Upstairs?"

What was her name? "Persimmon, or Pumpkin, or Prunella - I think. Last name is Parks. You'll love her, she's a hoot too."

"Yeah. Anybody else?"

"No."

"What are you doing outside wearing your inside clothes?"

"I was coming down to get my morning paper. Wanted to find out if Joe Louis--"

"Made quick work of Schmeling."

"He did?"

"Yeah." The detective scanned the sidewalk along the wall and the steps. "So, where are they?"

"What round? Where are what?"

"Two minutes in. The newspapers."

"Wha... You're pullin' my leg. Two minutes?"

"Schmeling's bunch threw in the towel. I'm not seeing any newspapers."

My mind tried to reenact the lightning fight with scanty information and also to locate the absent pile of the morning Post. "Now, how did I miss that?"

"Miss what?" The detective cocked his head to one side and was studying my confusion.

"The newspapers. They weren't here when I came out. This Joe ought to be on top of them up there on the steps. He's laying down here..."

He turned without acknowledging I'd been a big help and motioned for his sidekick. "Griz. Stiff got any identification? Officer Boggs! Go find a call box and send for the police surgeon. You!" He pointed at the patrolman. "Straddle that deathtrap and go find the paperboy."

"Yes, sir." The young cop departed as instructed with a spin of rubber on the pavement.

"Wallet in his inside coat pocket," announced Griz Asher. "Okay, here's something. Name's Jerry O'Dell. Address is lower Capital Hill."

"Ever seen him before, Sergeant?"

"Yeah, I think I have. Lives with that strange duck who's always sending us letters telling us how to do our job."

"Arcadia Vyne. Now, there's one eccentric so-and-so." He puffed his pipe and turned to look at me in my bathrobe as if he could attach the words 'eccentric so-and-so' to me, but it wouldn't stick. "You two are a lot alike, Cooper."

"I doubt it."

"Ain't this guy his nephew?" Asher searched the decedent's vest and pulled out a card wallet. "Okay. This is the guy. He's a courier."

"I'll take those. Pay a visit to Vyne myself." The detective shuffled the deck. "Here's one says he's a PI too." Holding it to the tip of his nose he turned to see me with a whole new set of eyes. "Well, how about this little surprise, Cooper? You two get sideways on a case? Forming a club? Swapin' recipes? Know anything about the set of wrist jewelry he's wearing tied to that suitcase handle?"

"I--" never got to finish my smart remark as a scream to wake the dead, present company excepted, came from inside my apartment building. We all ran up the steps, wedged through the door, with Sergeant Griz Asher winning, and came face-to-face with Mrs. Hidalgo. She was pointing behind the stairs with one hand and trying to calm her crying baby with the other.

"What is it, lady?" Sergeant Asher snatched up the mangled green carriage. "Why you blowin' your wig? There somethin' in here?"

"How am I supposed to take my little Felipe to the park?" She poked a finger into Detective Raft's chest. "You better arrest some body, pronto. I pay good money for that. What is this place coming to?" She turned on her heels, caught sight of the corpse on the sidewalk, and fainted.

Luckily, I became the hero of the day when I caught the baby.

Two

Nobody says I have habits, but I do. At least a few. Mostly when it comes to mealtime. About two days after I'd hit town, literally on the wrong side of the tracks, I stumbled into this greasy spoon, half-starved, and the short-order behind the counter spots me a meal.

I don't forget things like that. So, unless I'm way out of the jurisdiction, I have three squares a day here at Pug's, except on Saturday mornings when I utilize a little electric two burner in my apartment. Pug is extra busy the first morn of the weekend, and he says he can stand to miss my business. Other than the aforementioned Saturday exception, his establishment is a top priority for me. As soon as the initial five spot from my first case landed in my palm, I made good on my debt and vowed to be a regular. That and the fact he hired me for my second case which nabbed the guy with the heavy thumb on the scales in the market on Wazee Street. Might have to sleep out under a tree if there's no dough for the rent, but I never want to have an empty belly again. It ain't healthy.

At Pug's suggestion, I let him handle the order. I think it's usually what he's cooked up extra, but I don't complain. More often than not, it's ham n' eggs for breakfast, stew or chili for lunch, and hot meatloaf with a mound of freshly whipped potatoes plus a slice of pie for supper. Monday and Thursday, it's apple. Tuesday, raisin. Wednesday and Friday, cherry. On the weekends, it's rhubarb. I live for the weekends and Pug's rhubarb pie.

My 'official' office is up in my apartment, next to the sink and the two burner. For 'unofficial' business, it's here in the third booth from the back at Pug's. I can get phone calls here. I can converse with a client with a modicum of privacy. I can take a nap. I can drink all of the coffee I want, providing I get up and fill it myself. No waitresses at Pug's. There's just Pug.

"Some fight last night, huh, Jonas?" The bright yellow rag polished circles on the counter. "Lewis must have fists of steel." The old man sniffed a knuckle under his flat nose and feigned a one-two combination at the sugar jar. "My days in the ring, I'd have given him a run."

"I have no doubts, Pug. Radio is on the fritz again. I missed the whole thing."

"Didn't last long."

"So I heard."

"Why didn't you come over and listen to the bout with me, Jonas?"

I left the booth and moved to a stool in front of the counter and filled my cup. "Figured you'd be asleep. You ain't no spring chicken, Pug, and this place doesn't open by itself in the mornings."

He grinned with a smile missing the third tooth from the right. "Kinda glad it went in the opening. I was out like a light soon after." Pug released a belly laugh. "Just like Schmeling! Out like a light. Oh, boy!"

The bell over the door jingled. My building super waddled in and perched on the stool adjacent.

"Evening, Pug. Jonas."

"Tumbles," we countered.

"Meatloaf tonight, Pug?"

"Double helping for you and the kid. Heard of some ugly doings out on your sidewalk."

The old circus clown played the sad sack. "That ape of a cop, Griz Asher, he spent half an hour in my sitting room. Kept asking, what did I see? Who did I know? I see nothing. I know nothing."

"Some poor slob in the middle of something." I turned a cup over for the unhappy man and filled it with some steaming comfort. "Pug's coffee cures what ails, Tumbles."

He nodded his thanks, downed the scalding liquid without a flinch, and pushed the cup toward me for a redo.

"Tumbles, how do you stand it so hot all at once?"

"Someday, my boy, I will tell you the long story."

The aroma of two plates of meatloaf, with promised double portions, appeared in front of us seconds before the real deal. We both grabbed forks and dug into mashed potatoes with gusto when the two bells on top of the old wall phone interrupted our ecstasy, but only for a second.

More patrons entered and Pug hesitated to ignore them for the call.

"I'll get it." I motioned at the ringing box with my fork.

"Thanks, Jonas."

They were regulars who could seat themselves. But not in Pug's establishment. It just wasn't done.

So, I slid off the stool and answered the call on the old oak box. "Pug's place," I said into the mouthpiece voicing my best fake Italian. "*Signor Pugarelli* is with clientele, may you leave a message?"

"Is this Cooper? Jonas Cooper?"

"Lousy accent and all. Who's asking?"

"I'm calling on behalf of Mr. Arcadia Vyne."

"You are?"

"Yes, sir. My name is, Rodrick."

"And who, Mr. Rick, is Mr. Arcadia Vyne?"

"Rodrick, sir. My name is Rodrick."

"I stand corrected. Question stands as presented."

"He is in need of your private detective services and desires an audience with you at seven sharp."

I had to lean to the end of the cord to get a glance at the clock next to the menu board. Fifteen past six. I considered the summons and returned to the mouthpiece. This guy sounded British. Very exact. Very 'cheerio' and such. "How many people do I need to bring with me to fill out this audience?"

"Just yourself, Mr. Cooper. Shall I send a car for you?"

"I don't drive since the accident."

"It will have a chauffeur, I assure you. You will not be required to navigate."

"Where's this chariot taking me?"

"Lower Capitol Hill."

"Got a trolley stop nearby? Bus?"

"Yes, sir. We are within a block of tracks. The #11."

"I'll hoof it there myself. What's that address?"

"1007 Pennsylvania Street."

I pulled a pencil from my jacket and wrote the info on the wall next to other very important things. "This Vyne. He talk like you?"

"I beg your pardon, sir?"

"Is he from out of town, if you know what I mean? Do I need to bring an interpreter along, or will you do the honors?"

"He is an American, Mr. Cooper. Heir to the Vyne Tea Company."

"Oh, *that* Arcadia Vyne."

"Yes, sir."

"I'll be there at seven. Sharp."

"Very well, sir. Thank you."

The connection clicked close and I landed the earpiece on the hook. Then, I turned to Pug at the counter. "You ever heard of the Vyne Tea Company?"

"Sure. But, I don't serve it."

"Why not."

Pug lifted his personal coffee mug and held out his pinkie. "That's why."

"Not your usual crowd, huh?"

"I can't break their C-notes. Those rich ones up Capital Hill way, they think they got class. Full of hot air, if you ask me. The lot of 'em."

"Even this Arcadia Vyne guy, Tumbles?"

"Him? The strangest one of all. Moved into the John Good's castle smack in the middle of Quality Hill after his wife died, maybe two years ago. Heard he doesn't have anything to do with the Tea Company. His old maid sister, she has all the business sense. Leastwise the papers say."

"Is that so?"

"I'd steer clear of him, Jonas."

"Why, Tumbles?"

"He's right, Jonas."

"You too, Pug? What's the gag?"

Tumbles forked the last of the meatloaf into his mouth and reached for his saucer of rhubarb pie. "Anybody goes into this house of his... Don't come out no more."

THREE

One thing regarding the Mile High City is its downtown doesn't sit square with the rest of the real estate. Kinda like back home. Correspondingly, the Vyne mansion at 10th and Pennsylvania, south of the capitol building, didn't square with anything I'd ever seen in the domicile category.

Constructed of sandstone, the massive structure stood under a matching red tile roof. From the street I counted at least four chimneys. The entrance doors were heavy and detailed in intricate bronze and wrought ironwork. A brass turnkey doorbell warned the occupants of my arrival.

A butler of the mute variety greeted me with a nod and escorted me into a room with a sort of a semi-circular area on the Pennsylvania side. I parked my hat on a hall tree and surveyed the twenty-one narrow floor-to-ceiling windows. Every few feet a small table, with one chair to a table, faced its corresponding window. On each table sat a game of some sort. Most had chess boards with a war in progress, fourteen in all. Three more had backgammon, two checkerboards, a domino setup in a complex configuration, and one I couldn't identify. It appeared to be Oriental. Next to each game lay either a telegram or a handwritten note. An old Underwood in the corner held a sheet of half typed paper.

The second most obvious thing about the room consisted of cats. Lots and lots of cats. Paintings of cats. Carvings of cats. Cat figurines. Cat frescos and tapestries. The area above the fireplace showcased an oil portrait of a pleasant, big-boned lady, cat on lap. Centered amid all of this, on a large oak desk - a genuine and much alive cat. Black as coal curled up on a white paper blotter. Asleep.

The king of the castle stood on the fourth rung of a twelve rung ladder, reaching for a thick book on a shelf of thick books. The whole wall, also of semi-circular arrangement opposite the windowed side of the room, sported more volumes than I'd ever seen in a non-public area. The tall man I assumed to be a near cousin of Ichabod Crane as if described to life by Washington Irving himself. Skeletal face, pointed bent nose, thin hair combed straight back over his boney noggin. He wore a white lab coat with an assortment of paraphernalia protruding out of each pocket. To be precise - a stethoscope and a magnifying glass in one. A pipe and tobacco pouch string out of another. A rolled up document and a pair of white gloves in the third. From the chest pocket he removed half-moon reading glasses and perched them on the tip of his nose. "Mr. Cooper, I presume."

"Mr. Vyne, I presume."

He cocked his head toward the book. "Did you know, Mr. Cooper, there are recent discoveries of fossils buried vertically in four or more sections of rock?"

"No, I hadn't really thought about it."

"Fascinating study. Trees in Nova Scotia in layers extending upward more than two thousand feet! How is it possible? Wood rots when exposed to the elements. It doesn't fossilize. Hence these trees were preserved quickly. Rapid deposit of layers. Polystrate fossils embedded in layered rocks!"

"And your point, Mr. Vyne?"

"A discussion for another time." He nodded at the butler. "Thank you, Stewart. All for now."

The silent man faded out the doorway.

"My man thinks you're an idiot, Mr. Cooper. Are you an idiot?"

"That guy?" I threw a thumb over my shoulder. "The one with a voice like Harold Lloyd?"

"Stewart is a valet. I'm speaking of my secretary, Mr. Rodrick. He phoned you for this appointment."

"Idiot, huh?" The funny talker's stock just plummeted with me. "Not that I'm aware of."

"Detective Raft also took exception to your intellect. Something concerning inappropriate dress at a murder scene."

"When did you speak to Raft? I had the impression he took a shine to me."

"This afternoon."

"Murder happens fast, Mr. Vyne, and sometimes you don't have time to put on a tux."

He pursed his lips. "A tad flippant aren't we, Mr. Cooper? Young Jerry was my nephew. He may have traveled a great deal and we didn't see him often, but he will be missed."

"Sorry. It's bad business all around."

Do you play chess, Mr. Cooper?" He studied the cover of the book in his free hand.

"No."

He returned his gaze and peered at me over the top of the spectacles. "Are you willing to learn?"

For some reason I sensed this to be an interview question and my answer would either land me a job or expedite me to the door. I considered carefully. Mostly for effect. "Yes."

"Third table to your left, Mr. Cooper. Black is in check. What shall I do?"

I strolled over to the game and studied the layout. Half of the figures sat off the board. "What are these? Indians?"

"Mayans vs. Spaniards. Carved from malachite. Next move please."

"Which ones are black? The green ones or the beige ones?"

"The Mayans. Green."

"Oh." I studied the battle. The tallest one appeared to be the Chief of the lot. With careful reverence as seemed appropriate in the circumstance, and with absolutely no idea what I was doing, I slid the tall guy one square to the left. "That'll do."

Vyne, still clinging to the ladder with the crook of his left arm, fished a small pair of opera glasses from the pocket holding the stethoscope, flicked out a handle, and raised them in front of his peepers.

"Astounding!"

"I did good?"

"You chose the one losing option."

The cat on the blotter awoke with a large yawn, stood, arched its back to the limit, and hopped from the desk to the side chair and down to my feet. It did a figure-eight between my ankles and purred with content.

"Caffeine likes you, Mr. Cooper."

So, the chess match wasn't the interview breaker. The cat's approval was.

The spindly man pocketed the opera glasses, shelved the book, and descended to the floor. "Are you available to begin immediately, Mr. Cooper?" He motioned for me to take the padded side chair and settled into the banker's seat behind the desk. Something creaked. Might have been the chair, or him.

"Begin what, Mr. Vyne? Your summons lacked details."

He leaned forward and placed his elbows on the blotter and his angular chin on the knuckles of his bony clasped hands. "I may be mistaken in thinking you're the man for the job."

"You want me to find out who killed your nephew in front of my apartment building." I retreated into the padding of my chair and crossed my legs. "Sorry,

Mr. Vyne. I'm not sure what you've heard about me, but I'm strictly business related. Some domestic, but no spying on the spouse stuff. None of the hard crime for me anymore. Had enough for one lifetime back on the force."

Vyne smiled and leaned further forward on his elbows. "Then, you don't know."

Caffeine, appeared in my lap, circled twice, and nested. "Know what?"

"Interesting." He lifted his chin from his clasped hands, brushed a bit of Caffeine's hair from the blotter and reclined with a creak. "As I said, I had a visit from Detective Burgess Raft this afternoon. Remarkably complex man, this Raft. Often wrong in his methods, but a bulldog determination to get to the bottom of things. Yes, I'm aware of the shooting in front of your apartment, Mr. Cooper. With a bit of insistence on my part, the good detective told me Jerry O'Dell, my nephew, was the fourth private detective killed this month. Who knows, Mr. Cooper? You may be slated for number five."

Then and there I decided I needed to be reading more than the sports page and the daily want ads.

Four

Due to the lateness of the hour, all of nine o'clock, my new client, Arcadia Vyne, insisted I spend the night in the fourth apartment over the carriage house. Rick occupied one of the two facing the drive. Baylee, the chauffeur, the second, next door. Up the back stairs, which divided into two flights, I found the final residence of Jerry O'Dell and another flat for myself. Rick had given me a key to both, so I decided to check out the O'Dell digs before turning in. Since the D.T.C. runs 'til ten, I could have taken it back to my place, but for some reason this seemed the better course of action.

O'Dell, the nephew, kept a neat apartment. Organized to such a point all his socks lined up like soldiers in the chest of drawers.

A roll top desk proved appealing and the lock necessitated picking. I plopped in the chair, switched on a green glass reading lamp, and perused some opened correspondence. The first letter was a request for O'Dell to courier some business papers for one of the law firms downtown. Apparently routine, as the request contained the wording 'per your usual fee' near the salutation. The next envelope held an assortment of assignments up for grabs from a clearing house in New York. The pay looked good on some of them and I pocketed the pages for possible leads after this affair ran its course. More envelopes expelled receipts for train fare to and from New York City with arrival early this morning, a ticket stub from the Tabor Opera House, and a refund check for three dollars and twenty-two cents from a mail order company.

The remainder of the apartment revealed nothing interesting. I studied the other key and debated on whether to take the offer to stay. Compensation hadn't been discussed yet and if nothing came of it, at least I'd have the satisfaction of lodging in a room with a set of towels that matched.

Around two o'clock in the morning something woke me in the little apartment over the carriage house. The door closing. It took a few minutes for me to determine if whoever passed through it was on the other side or currently standing at the foot of my bed in the dark.

I switched on the bedside lamp.

Next to the night table sat a chair. It hadn't been there when I went to sleep. No one had sat in it watching me. I knew this because my trousers were hung neatly over the back, under my coat and vest. They were cleaned and pressed. My suspenders were rolled in a coil. Unlike the crumpled pile in the floor they occupied three hours earlier. My shoes, formerly scuffed and soiled, resided next to one of the chair's legs with a polish keen enough for me to see myself peering over the edge of the bed at them. My tie, folded on the cushion. My hat... "Where's my hat?"

It must have been either Silent Stewart or Rick the secretary. Maybe someone else. And why weren't there any females working in this house?

I didn't like the idea of someone being in my room while I slept. Friend *or* foe. Even if, technically, the premises didn't belong to me. In my line of work folks who play sneaky can get themselves hurt.

FIVE

Breakfast in the Vyne mansion proved disappointing. Hot tea in a fancy cup of which I couldn't get my finger through the handle and some toast with marmalade. The master of the house sat across from me with Rick on my left and Baylee, a short stocky boy no more than twenty years old, on my right. Silent Stewart stood at the ready, but with his own tea cup in white gloved hand. At least Arcadia Vyne didn't come across as so snooty he didn't let the help dine with him. Then again upon further contemplation as I soaked it all in, and with my inadequate knowledge of how the snooty upper-class should in fact behave, I decided this in certain circles might be categorized as not the norm.

Vyne sipped his tea and pointed a nibbled slice of toast in my direction. "Mr. Cooper, please describe the scene of my nephew's demise. In detail if you don't mind."

I caught the veiled smiles traded by the butler, the chauffeur, and whatever Rick was. "In detail?"

"If you please."

"Very well." I dabbed marmalade from my lip with a linen napkin and spilled the whole grizzly story.

When I'd finished, I sat back and waited for the response.

Silence.

"Well?"

"Surely, you can do much better, Mr. Cooper!"

The help suppressed their own respective chuckles behind their own respective linen napkins.

"That will do, boys."

I leaned forward. "What's the gag, *boys*?"

"You have failed to tell me anything I don't already know, Mr. Cooper. Detective Raft volunteered numerous details you've neglected to report. If you are to call *yourself* a detective, you will certainly need to do better. Much, much better. Now. Again. From the start."

"Of all of the..." I took a deep breath. "Okay." In my mind I envisioned this updated delivery like a pitcher on the mound staring down DiMaggio. After letting them have it, I once again settled back with the confidence of someone who just pitched a no-hitter.

Silence.

"Oh now, come on!" I stood and glared at the group. "Do you want me to draw it on the wall for you? Give me a pencil."

Rick held up an index finger and nodded. "If I may, sir. I'll try to enlighten Mr. Cooper."

"Certainly, Rodrick." Vyne's face reveled no emotion from behind his cup. "I think someone should."

The secretary motioned for me to follow him from the dining room and put his hand on my shoulder. "Mr. Cooper. Mr. Vyne is extremely detail orientated. His mind is a logic machine. Give him the facts. In order. Without commentary. A. B. C. 1. 2. 3."

"You guys are a tree full of nuts."

Rick reached into his vest pocket and extracted a check with my name on it. "Identify the killer of Mr. O'Dell and I'm instructed to give this to you."

The paper sported a five and more zeros than I'd seen in a year.

"What's the gag?"

"No gag, Mr. Cooper."

"Were you in my room early this morning?"

"Your clothes were a mess. Mr. Vyne instructed Stewart to--"

Explained why I didn't hear anything. "Stunts like that will get Stewart shot."

"He also took the liberty of cleaning your gun."

"He... What?"

"Filthy, I'm told. We're surprised it didn't--"

"Forget it." I took a deep breath, watched the check go back into the vest pocket, and retraced our steps to the breakfast table. Earlier I hadn't noticed the beautiful landscaped garden beyond the windows. I suddenly understood the kind of detail Vyne required.

Returning to my chair, I slowly lifted the teacup and sipped. Not bad, for something watered down, I suppose. This time I told it in a different way. Lining up my A's with my 1's and my C's with my 3's. I even included the part about spiriting the officer's gun into the gutter.

For the first time Arcadia Vyne smiled. "Much better, Mr. Cooper. You've almost got it."

I threw my napkin across the room. "For Pete's..."

Rick cleared his throat. "Maybe Mr. Cooper can tell us what he discovered in Mr. O'Dell's quarters last evening."

Envelope by envelope, I unfolded the inventory.

Arcadia Vyne popped the last bit of toast into his mouth and stood. "Satisfactory. Rodrick, as it is Sunday, take the list tomorrow and cross reference it to any courier jobs in New York. Allow for the time difference and call the ones you discover. Ask them if my nephew took any of their assignments. Mr. Cooper. The list, if you please."

I surrender the papers. "What am I to do?"

Vyne stood. "We are off to church, Mr. Cooper. You are welcome to join us, if you like. Tomorrow morning Baylee will be at your disposal to drive you anywhere you want to go. Begin by going back to the sidewalk in front of your apartment and memorize the details. Check in with Rodrick to see what he has found out from New York."

"Why don't you just go with me? If it's details you want to see."

"Important work to do in the morning. I'm expecting core samples from the western part of the state tomorrow afternoon and I need to prepare my laboratory." With this he marched out the door.

No surprise to me if he stocked a lab. Probably in the basement behind his little toy train sets.

Rick followed Vyne, then Baylee, then Silent Stewart.

I surveyed the empty nook. "Church?"

Six

Bright and early Monday morning, minus a laundry visit in the night (because I'd propped a chair under the door knob), and sans breakfast, I took the trolley with Baylee's promise to meet me later at my building on 17th.

"You own a camera, Baylee Boy?" I'd asked the young man on the way out the back door of the Vyne mansion.

"No."

"Got any folding green on you?"

"A little."

"Swell." I handed him a scrap of paper with an address and a name on it. "Swing by this shop I know. Buy a Brownie from the guy and get him to teach you how to use it."

"Why?"

"If it's detail Vyne wants, it's detail he's gonna get."

The trolley ride conveyed me to the Denver Public Library, situated in the Civic Center district and a stone's throw from the #6 stop.

There's this librarian with blue peepers I know who sits behind the main desk. Her name's Mary Smith. Yes, that is her name. Mary is cute with dimples and we've gone Dutch a couple of times at Pug's. I secured her agreement to help with some research on the O'Dell case, with a promise to pick up the whole tab this evening and even throw in some pie to boot.

Mary relinquished her stool to a subordinate and led me to the newspaper files, shushing and giving the stink eye to several patrons along the way.

Once there, she expertly rounded up stories which pertained to three other private detectives who'd been murdered recently.

"Here we go." Her voice whispered over the table like cream from a pitcher. "Victim number one. Tobias Watkins. Stabbed in the throat. A week ago. Early morning. Sidewalk in front of the opera house at 16th & Curtis."

"Well, there's one similarity and one not." I jotted the info into my notebook.

"How so?"

"Early morning. Bit earlier. Different means."

"Oh."

"Does it say what kind of case he was on?"

"No. I don't see anything here."

"Guess I'll have to sweet talk Raft. Next?"

She shuffled papers. "Next morning. Rio Richards. Poisoned cup of coffee at Union Station. He was waiting for a client to arrive from Chicago."

"Seems our bird likes to get the worm before breakfast."

"He certainly has a diverse repertoire."

I glanced about for a dictionary, but my expression must have given me away.

"He likes to kill in a variety of ways."

"Yes, I'm picking up on that."

The next story, of a killing the day prior to O'Dell's, told of the demise of Jake 'the Candyman' Caine. Someone had dropped a small piece of a building on him just before daylight.

"Part of the Kittredge's seventh story broke away from the top of the fire escape, landing on Caine who was standing in an alleyway," read Mary. "Known for his reputation with the ladies and also for nosing in businesses on both sides of the law, sources at police headquarters stated they weren't surprised he'd met his end."

"Four private eyes and four kinds of murder. All the same song with different verses."

"Jonas, are you in danger?" Mary blinked her big blues at me.

"Well, probably. But, not from knives, poison, guns, or buildings. Those have all been claimed already."

SEVEN

Baylee pulled to the curb in front of the apartment building in a shiny Packard. As he slid from the seat, he cocked the chauffeur's cap back on his noggin.

"Nice car." I gestured toward the green roadster. "Bet it set your boss back a tea bag or two."

"900 Light Eight Roadster. Only built 'em in '32."

"And he lets you run around in it?"

"Jerry O'Dell borrowed my regular tin can. A '36." Baylee yanked open the passenger door and extracted a funny looking black box with the price tag still attached.

"That ain't like no Brownie I've ever seen."

"Better. This set me back three checkers. Called a Bullet. Guy showed me how to load the film and what to do." Baylee presented it for my approval. "Said if I got back within the hour, he'd develop our pictures before supper."

"We'll see. Won't we?" I pointed out several vantage points. "Get a couple of shots from each spot. Be back in a few. Gonna run into Pug's and call Rick to see what he's found out from New York. Coffee?"

The little man nodded and went about his business like a tourist in a foreign country.

A jingle of the bell told Pug of my arrival and by habit he grabbed the coffee pot with the hem of his apron. When I held up two fingers and pointed at the door, he poured two paper cups.

On the second ring, Rick answered. "Arcadia Vyne residence."

"Hey, Rick. It's me. Whatca find out?"

"Rodrick, Mr. Cooper. Rodrick."

"Got it. What about N.Y.?"

The secretary sighed. "Mr. O'Dell took an assignment for the firm of Henrich, Montgomery, and Clay. He was to deliver a packet here in Denver the morning of his demise."

"And what kind of firm is this Montgomery and Clay bunch?"

"Architectural design."

"Say again?"

"They draft blueprints for municipal buildings, land tracts, and subdivisions."

"Oh. Good work, Rick."

"Rod... I give up."

"Hang in there. Thanks for the info." I jotted this new information in my notebook, planted some change on the counter for Pug, and tracked down Baylee Boy with his new toy.

"How's it going?"

"Okay, I guess." He accepted the coffee and pointed. "Still need to get a few from across the street."

"You snap one from the entrance up there? Facing out this way?"

"Not yet."

I eyed the two holes in the door and still wondered how O'Dell's body got from there to here. "And the sidewalk?" I pointed at his shoes.

"First thing."

"Great. Think I'll run inside and swap a clean undershirt."

"You want me to wait for you?"

"No. Shake a leg back to the camera shop and get those photos developed. I'll catch a trolley or a bus."

Baylee tipped his cap and headed across the street.

"Hey!" I yelled after him. "Move your car out of the way first."

"Right."

With the thought of a fresh shirt and a shave, I went up the steps and entered the foyer. Mrs. Hidalgo's baby carriage still lay in shambles next to the stairs. Maybe I could get Vyne to replace it for her.

Up in my apartment I scratched the stubble off of my chin and worked my arms into my other clean undershirt just as the piano and clarinet of *Body and Soul* filtered their way through the ceiling.

A bit of tonic slicked my hair back nicely and with a splash of aftershave behind each ear I felt presentable and ready to pay a visit to the dame on the third floor. As I finished tying the knot in my tie I ascended to her landing two steps at a time and banged on the door with my fist.

"What is it!" she squawked when the door flew open. "Oh, it's you. Too loud again?"

The song changed. "Can I come in?" I yelled over the new beat of clarinet and drums.

She cinched her flowery robe around her waist and pushed a bob of red hair back into place with the palm of her hand. "What for?" She yelled back.

"I need to ask you some questions."

"Questions about what?"

"Saturday morn's shooting."

"I already talked to the cops." She reached to her right and lifted the needle from the platter on the portable's turntable. "Didn't realize you were a cop too."

"Who said I was a cop?" Too loud. "Um. Who said..." This time not so much.

"You carry a gun."

"How'd you know that?" I absently adjusted my coat.

"I've seen it on you."

"I'm not a cop. Private detective."

"PI?"

"Yes."

"Let me see your badge."

"Don't carry a badge. Here's my card."

She studied the little paper overture. "Jonas Cooper. Private Investigations. Denver, Colorado. Well. Finally, a formal introduction."

Still didn't know her full name. "Since we're being formal, you are?"

She held out a hand with chewed nails. Sign of the nervous type. "Prunella Parks. Pleasure to meet you, I'm sure."

Her grip was solid and I noticed her fingertips betrayed smudges of charcoal or something on them.

"May I come in?"

"I suppose. Place is a mess. I work out of here, you know."

"No, I didn't know."

She stepped back far enough for me to enter the apartment and her line of work immediately became apparent.

"You're an artist?"

"An illustrator."

Various easels occupied the room. Each with a work in progress, all sketches started in pencil. A large pad of paper lay open over the coffee table with the outline of a woman's face.

"What kind of drawings are these?"

"Advertising. For magazines." She picked up the pad and a pencil. Her hand made a flourish over the paper.

Yes, it was clear now. I'd seen this type of work often. "You've got a talent."

"Thanks. It pays the bills." She drew some more.

I leaned in to peer at a finished work, a framed page from a familiar magazine, hanging on the wall over the record player. The style was identical to the other drawings about the room, however the signature didn't say 'Prunella Parks' but something else. "This you as well?"

She laughed. "The big advertisers all live in the dark ages. They won't buy anything drawn by a woman. So, I sign them that way. They think I'm a man. They're in New York. I'm here. Nobody's any the wiser."

"You don't have to visit them?"

"No." Her pencil shaded something on the paper. "Got 'em convinced I'm a bit eccentric and as long as they like the work, they don't push it."

"How's the pay?"

"I do all right." She offered me a seat on the couch and a drink. I took the former and declined the latter, remembering my abandoned cup of coffee on the counter down in my apartment.

"Suit yourself, sweetie. Now, what do you want to know? I already told that bear from the police everything." She scowled as something came to mind. "Saturday morning. You yelled at me!"

"It needed to be done."

"I would've called the cops. But, I didn't have a nickel."

"They found out anyway."

"I suppose." Prunella Parks tilted her head and continued to draw. "Was he shooting at you?"

"I don't think so."

"The guy who caught it down on the sidewalk?"

"Looks like it."

"Poor sap. Probably in the wrong place at the wrong time."

"That's what I'm trying to find out."

"You on the case?"

"I am."

"You charge much?"

"Depends. You got something for me after I'm done with this?"

"Naw."

I shrugged it off. "What I really want to ask you concerns the delivery you expected. Did it ever come?"

Her eyebrows arched. "Now, you mention it... No." She scratched the side of her head with the nub end of the pencil. "Guess I forgot all about it."

"So, I'm assuming it wasn't anything important."

She cradled the pad under her chin, leaned forward, and lowered her voice. "Here's the thing. I got a telegram telling me to anticipate a package. I never get packages, I only send them out."

"Where was this package coming from?"

"New York."

"Don't your clients in New York send you things?"

"Not by courier."

"By courier?"

"Yeah, the telegram said by courier."

"Can I see it?"

"Threw it away."

It figured. I remembered the refuse out back wouldn't be picked up until late afternoon. So, it might be worth a visit. "This telegram, seem odd?"

"Well, yeah. We never correspond that way. Always through the mail. Nothing is ever urgent."

"Have you heard of..." I checked my notes. "Henrich, Montgomery, and Clay?"

"No. Who are they, sweetie? Bunch of shysters?"

"It's not important. You'll clue me if your package ever arrives?" I stood and put the notebook back in my inner jacket pocket.

She grabbed my lapels and pulled me in close, the drawing pad between us. "Sure thing, sugar. You will come and see me again, sometime, won't you? Now, we've been properly introduced and all." She leaned away.

I reached to tilt the pad to see what she'd drawn. A waltzing Fred Astaire - with *my* face. A pretty good likeness at that. "This supposed to be me?"

"All in fun, sweetie. All in fun. You can take me dancing some day, you know."

"Tickets to the Denver Club's New Year bash are in your future."

"Too swanky."

"Rainbow Ballroom?"

"Seven months out. But, a date's a date."

I backpedaled to the door, lowered the needle to the still spinning groove of the platter, and pointed at the sketch. "Frame it for me, will ya?"

"It'll cost extra!" she yelled after me as I waltzed to the music all the way to ground level.

A trot around to the alley brought me to the refuse cans, brimmed with possibilities. Twenty minutes later, and with the help of a nosey little mutt, I found the telegram rolled up in a discarded pencil sketch of a man drinking bubbly from a ladies slipper. The person it was addressed to proved enlightening.

Upon my return to the street in front of the apartment, I whistled for Baylee to finish his sightseeing. "You still here? Get some good ones?"

"Time will tell, boss." He fell into step with me. "What now?"

"You got me bugged about O'Dell's car. Did you spot it anywhere around here?"

"No. With those bright orange fenders and black body it sticks out like a pelican in a chicken coop."

I extended a paw to stop him and studied up and down the street and across the way. "Which is faster to police HQ? Bus or trolley?"

"Save your nickel. I'll drop you off on my way back to get this film developed." Baylee headed for his Packard.

While I waited for him to circle around, I had time to think about returning early in the morning to catch the paperboy. Maybe he saw something.

EIGHT

Detective Burgess Raft's desk dominated the end of a long room of desks on the second floor of the Denver Police Station. It faced outward with neat stacks of work in several different piles. Organized and ready. I'm sometimes the mischievous sort and considered doing some shuffling for kicks, but thought better of it seeing how I needed information with no irritation.

Besides, Griz Asher's smaller desk occupied a space on the floor a few feet away. Not as neat. Not as much a target for mischief, but more deserving. So, while I waited for Raft, I turned all of the sergeant's pencils upside down in their cup.

"I'd keep my nose out of other people's business," grunted Raft as he approached from my blindside. "Especially guys with bigger knuckles than mine."

"Afternoon." I grabbed a chair and straddled it, with my chest against the back. "Any progress on the O'Dell shooting?"

"Some." He parked his hat on a wall hook.

"Want to share?"

"Not particularly." Raft sat and searched his upper drawer. "You been in here?"

"No, sir, I have not."

The curved pipe appeared in his hand and he seemed satisfied with my answer. "Heard you went to work for Vyne. Better watch out around that teeto-taler. Guy's a nut in my book."

"You may be right. I'm looking for one of his cars."

"You are. Business must be slow for you."

"Packard. Bright orange fenders. Last driven by Jerry O'Dell."

"You don't say."

"Find any double-parked where they aren't sup-posed to be?"

The detective packed the bowl of his pipe with to-bacco from a pouch, nestled back in his chair, and put his feet cross-ankle on the desk. "Hey! Lester!"

At the other end of the room a voice responded.

"Go downstairs. See if anyone on patrol has spotted a Packard with orange fenders parked where it's not supposed to be."

"Black with orange fenders," I added.

"Yes, sir!" volleyed the voice.

Raft lit the pipe with a match and waited for the smoke to spiral over his head. "Had another PI make a reservation for the morgue this morning." He said it like he'd just told me he bought a new hat to replace the one on the hook.

"What? Where?"

"Sloan's Lake. But our killer added a new twist."

"Such as..."

"This one, Pinky Bronson, got himself drowned. Must be open season on you guys."

"You don't seem to be losing any sleep over it."

"Most times you so-called 'private eyes' get in my way."

"We gotta turn a buck or two to pay for the shoes we wear out. Where exactly is this body of water Pinky tried to inhale?"

"23rd & Lakeside." Raft held his pipe in the cup of his hand and chewed on his lip. "Something about you, Cooper. Ever wear a badge?"

"I did. East of here."

"You say that like a whole lot of story goes along."

I shrugged. "There is, but I don't converse the matter."

"Fair enough." The detective took a long puff and again leaned back in his chair.

"You pull any slugs out of my stairwell?"

The detective nodded.

"And?"

"Two .38s. Rough shape wounds. I'm guessing .38 specials. Doc Wallace, the police surgeon, says the one that went through O'Dell's neck was nasty enough to kill, but didn't. Both came from low and close in."

"The step to the back of the head then?"

"You picked up on that?"

"I did."

Raft nodded as if impressed. "Under the circumstances, and I'm referring to your competition dying all over town, I'm going to cut you some slack, Cooper." He tapped the desk with the stem of his pipe. "There's a little file here under my nose. Don't let Griz see you reading it. We haven't had any luck finding case information. You guys keep lousy files. Help yourself to the photos. Might come in handy, but I want them returned pronto. And put the file back precisely the way you found it. Understand? Or, I tell Griz who moved his pencils."

While I absorbed this new information, the runner returned from downstairs and handed the detective a piece of paper.

He nodded his thanks, pulled his feet off the desk, and passed the report for my perusal.

"Black Packard, orange fenders," he confirmed. "Parked in front of the new City and County Building. Two flat tires."

"Within walking distance of my apartment."

"Within walking distance of your apartment. I'd be watching my back if I were you."

NINE

Baylee retrieved me in front of the station on his way back from the camera shop. We'd found the borrowed car and made arrangements for the flats to be repaired. Thereafter, we pegged a man who'd seen O'Dell in the halls of the City and County Building. Raft's file had given me a page of notes and three photos. The one of our boy we showed around. A custodian flagged it and remembered seeing O'Dell outside the City Planning Office on Saturday morning.

"It was all locked up."

"What do you mean?" I handed the pictures over to Baylee and stared the janitor in the eye.

"Planning Office was closed for some reason. It's always open on Saturday morning."

"Out to lunch maybe?"

"No, sir. Too early. There was a note on the door."

"What did it say?"

"Didn't read it."

Figured. "O'Dell read it?"

"Guy in the snap? Yeah, he read it. Took it off the nail and stuck it in his case."

"The Planning Office open now?"

"Sure. At least the secretary is there."

"How do you know?"

The janitor lowered his voice and tilted his head. "She's a looker. Don't nobody miss seeing her."

"She here Saturday morning?"

"Like I said, not a soul in that office. Not all day."

I thanked the man and whispered for Baylee to slip him two bits while I visited the looker in the Planning Office.

A knock on the door solicited an invite to enter and sure enough, behind the desk sat a tomato husbands would never tell their wives about. The wooden placard introduced her as Miss P. Baxter and I made an extra mental note of the name.

An inner office door stood open to my right and two men emerged at the end of a joke and slapping each other on the back. The taller of the two, with a head full of salty hair and matching regent mustache, sized me up. "You need help? What's he want, Phyllis?"

"I don't know, Mr. Harmon." She pointed her nail file at me. "He just came in."

Harmon turned to his colleague, a wiry guy with a gray bowtie. "Downhill all the way now, Chester. It's downhill all the way. Nothing more to worry on the subject." Then to me. "Be with you in a minute."

The two departed into the hallways of the City and County Building.

"Nice guy." I removed my hat. "Phyllis, is it?"

"What do ya want?" Apparently courtesy was not a skill anyone in this office knew.

"Who was that?" I threw a thumb over my shoulder at the door.

"Mr. Harmon is the City Planner. Mr. Chester is a developer. Chester Estates is one of his. He's been in the papers. What concern is it of yours?"

I shook my head. "No concern, really. Do you have any city maps?"

"Sure, why didn't ya say so?" She pointed at a rack of literature on the wall with the file. One on the right has all of the bus and trolley routes on it."

"Thanks." I grabbed one, shoved it into my inner

coat pocket, and noticed one of the maps had been pinned to the wall above the rack. Two sections of town were circled in red. One identified as 'Adams Acres' west of Overland Park and the other marked 'The Chester Country Club' southwest of the Platte River and Alameda. Of the two, Adams Acres had a big X slashed across it. "Are you acquainted with a Mr. Jerry O'Dell?"

"No." Her blank stare conveyed I'd not caught her off guard, but she simply didn't register the name. She wasn't dumb. She just didn't seem to care.

"Okay, thought he might have been in here. On Saturday morning maybe?"

"Ask Mr. Harmon when he comes back."

"Were you here Saturday?"

"For your information, buster, I was given a day off. So, I took a ride with my boyfriend over to Red Rocks. What's it to ya?"

"Was Mr. Harmon in on Saturday?"

"What's with all the questions? Ya a reporter or somethin'?"

"No, not a reporter." I put my hat back on my head. "Merely a curious sort. Thanks for the map."

She held out a tin can. "Five cents."

TEN

They buried Jerry O'Dell in the Mount Prospect City Cemetery. A rough looking place with toppled monuments and overgrown weeds. When I say they, I mean uncle Arcadia Vyne and his sibling, Aurora. In front of the casket there were five chairs with Vyne sitting on one end and sister on the other with a space of three empty seats between. Two bookends huddled in their coats against the raw wind. The dreary and overcast sky hung above them to the extent the mountains were obscured from sight.

After serving as pall bearers, with a groundskeeper and the minister, Baylee Boy, Rick, Silent Stewart, and myself stood at a polite distance and waited.

"Didn't O'Dell have any friends?" I whispered.

"Kept to himself," offered Baylee. "Traveled a lot."

"The lady. Aurora. She's an odd duck. Mother?"

Rodrick stifled a jeer behind a gloved hand. "Hardly, sir. Miss Aurora Vyne is Mr. Vyne's older sister. Children of Albert and Adelia. Not on speaking terms for several years as you can see by the distance they are keeping between them. Miss Aurora arrived this morning from London, where she oversees the tea business, and has plans to depart just as quickly. The youngest, Alberta O'Dell, bore Gerald. In '34 she and her husband helped discover the world's largest tea bush in Ceylon. It had a diameter of twenty-four feet and a circumference of sixty-seven feet. They say four pounds of green leaf were plucked from it on that day. Shortly thereafter the O'Dells went into the Ceylon jungle and never came out."

"You're kidding."

"No, sir. They were searching for *Dan Cong Gold*, the definitive champagne of tea, and didn't return."

"Doesn't exist," chided Baylee. "It's a myth."

"You said the coffee-rust fungus of 1869 was a legend also." Rodrick made a *tsk tsk* sound.

"I never did! But, *Dan Cong Gold* simply doesn't exist. If it did it would grow in China, not Ceylon."

"The boss thinks it does."

"Do you mugs lie around dreamin' about this stuff at night?" I turned my collar up against the wind. "Vyne got any other family? Brothers?"

"One other sister, Ardith." Rodrick lowered his voice even more. "She's in the Agnes Memorial Sanatorium. Although, they're going to move her soon."

"Move her? Why?"

"Ardith is the last patient. Mr. Vyne has contributed to the original Phipps' endowment, but they won't keep it open for one. The Army Air Corps is renovating it for their technical school."

The minister appeared to be wrapping things up and our little group shuffled our feet in anticipation of leaving.

"You gents gonna miss Jerry O'Dell?" I asked.

The three looked at each other and nodded ever so slightly.

"Aware of anybody who wanted him dead?"

Three heads indicated the negative.

"Well somebody did," I said as I followed them to the cars. "And it may take all of us to find out who."

❦❦❦

Baylee placed his photos in a line across the front of Arcadia Vyne's desk. Some were out of focus. One conveyed a good shot of one of his shoes. Two or three had been obscured by a bus. The rest gave a fair, albeit skewed, representation of the scene of O'Dell's demise from four perspectives.

As the thin man sipped his tea he paced slowly, eyeing each pic in turn. All the while I gave him as detailed a report as I could of the day's encounters. I even left in the remark by Detective Raft on the subject of my new employer being a nut in his book.

"Have you visited any of the other murder sites?" Vyne pulled a magnifying glass out of his lab coat pocket and studied a photo of the front door.

"Not yet."

"Don't you think you should?"

"Maybe."

He swiveled his head, one large eye staring through the lens. "Maybe?"

I produced the map I'd procured at the City Planning Office and spread it out over the photos. With a pencil I slashed a cross mark at each site. "Your nephew shot, here in front of my apartment. 17th Street. Tobias Watkins stabbed. In front of the Opera House. 16th & Curtis. Rio Richards. Poison coffee. Union Station. Candyman Caine. Sky fell on him in an alley next to the Kittredge. Also on 16th. Pinky Bronson at Sloan's Lake. Hey, this is interesting!"

"What, Mr. Cooper?"

From under the map I retrieved an out of focus photo and dropped it between all the marks. "Professor, these places are near bus routes. A big loud bus blends into the scenery and a witness will never mention it."

"I am not a professor, Mr. Cooper."

"Sorry, I tend to hang names on folks when I meet them and they just sorta stick."

"It's very rude."

"Rude, huh?"

"Yes. If you are going to speak to someone, call them by the name they give you, not one you choose to give them."

"It's how I remember people. Keeps them all straight in my mind." My continued focus on the map and not on him brought silence. "What?"

"Let's ignore the map for a moment and talk about your methods."

"Who's the detective here?"

Vyne sighed and settled back into his reading chair. "Were you a good student, Mr. Cooper?"

I mulled the question for a moment and slid into the adjacent seat. Very comfortable. For sitting. Not comfortable for this conversation. "So - so, I guess."

"I can imagine." He put his hands on his knees and

leaned toward me. "When you tackled a subject in school. Tell me. How did you go at it?"

"Go at it?"

"Well, did you try to take in the big picture first?" He spread his arms wide, as if engulfing the room. "Or, did you attack it a piece at a time?"

"Well..." I shrugged. "I guess whatever seemed appropriate at the moment."

This statement appeared to really frustrate my interrogator. He huffed as his body regrouped back into the chair. A long boney index finger started to tap, tap, tap the leather. "Mr. Cooper. Let me tell you how I tackle a subject."

"If it will make you feel better."

He tilted his head back a bit. I could tell no one ever sassed him like this before. Or, if they had, it had been one of those sisters and he didn't like the memory.

"Mr. Cooper. Early on. In school. I loved the challenge of learning all about something, provided it sufficiently intrigued me. Given a new subject, I'd examine it from every conceivable angle. I didn't want to waste my time on getting half the story. Time is precious, Mr. Cooper. Do not forget it. Thus, having discerned the scope of the thing, I attacked it at the base level. Take math for instance. I did not move on from

1 + 1 = 2 to 1 + 2 = 3 until I took 1 + 1 = 2 apart to its fundamental basics."

"Well, if you can't get past 1 + 1--"

"You're missing the point, Mr. Cooper!" Vyne's fist slammed down onto the arm of the chair. "Focus on the fundamentals I am placing before you now. Listen to what I am saying. Take it apart. Put it back together. Take it apart again. See if it will go together some other way. Examine each piece. Look behind it. Look under it. Look beyond it. Look inside it. Can those pieces, parts, portions, sections, slices, sectors, fragments, bits, splinters, or chips be broken down further? Can they be--"

I waved him off. "If I did things like that, I'd be all day getting out the gate."

"Yes, Mr. Cooper. You have grasped a fundamental. But..." He stood and pointed at my nose. "But, when you leave the gate you will be as prepared as you can possibly be. You will be ready for any contingency. You will see when you get to 1 + 2 = 3, there is no doubt to the underlying deep-seated fact and truth of 1 + 1 = 2."

I stood and looked him in the eyes. Both of 'em. "That settles it then."

"Settles what, Mr. Cooper?"

"Like it or not. I'm callin' you 'Professor.'"

Eleven

I'd forgotten to put the chair in front of the door and woke to find my clothes once again ready for the day. Suddenly visions of 1 + 1 and 2 - 3 started dancing in my head.

"Oh, no you don't!" I yelled at the walls as I crawled off the bed and grabbed my pants. "It don't rub off on me that easy. I will work this case my way." I counted my shoes. "1 shoe + 1 more shoe = ... Oh, for Pete's sake!"

I still didn't like the thought of someone being in my room uninvited in the wee hours of the morn and I certainly didn't like the thought of Mr. Professor Arcadia Vyne messing with my mind at any time of the day *or* night. So, I decided to finish my slumber in my own bed, in my own apartment. Besides, it'd give me a chance to get out front early enough to question that paperboy.

❦

Loud music from upstairs.

I didn't remember any trumpets when my head hit the pillow for the second time.

I also didn't remember my pillowcase being over my head. Or, of two hammy sets of fingers around my throat.

So, I quickly began to form some new memories. Memories of kicking the guy in the shin with my big toe. Of grabbing him under both arms. New memories of his letting go and landing on the floor somewhere to my left. A fresh recollection of the pillowcase coming off my head, of it being dark, save for the bit of light from the window and the glint of said light off the knife blade coming at my face. To this I added an upper cut to where I thought his jaw might be, and the feeling of success as my knuckles cracked and his teeth gnashed. We grappled around for the next few minutes or so and managed to break almost every piece of furniture in the little room. Things crashed.

Things came apart. He clocked me over the head with Exhibit A. I countered with B. No one could have heard it over the din drubbing the ceiling. Had I always slept through such noise? I didn't have time to take this fragment of information, as Professor Vyne would have me do, apart to its core. I had a war to win. With renewed focus I took a deep breath and thrashed the darkness. My opponent contributed with a sudden rush. I might have deflected this charge if I hadn't caught one of my loose shoes under the heel of my left foot and fallen backward. I felt the blade of the knife slice up under my arm and stick in something behind me. Then it snapped. He must have thought he'd broken it off in me, because I heard the hilt bounce off the wooden floor as he made a quick exit.

Meanwhile the trumpet blared from the apartment above and drums joined in.

"Who listens to that stuff at..." I pushed myself up the dresser and located the light switch. My electric stove lay in pieces and I felt satisfaction knowing it had been Exhibit B. The clock was on its side at my elbow. One of the bells liberated. "Quarter after four. Good grief."

My clothes were in wads all over the place and one of my shoes sported a big scuff on the toe. Guess having someone clean 'em for you in the middle of the night might not be so bad after all.

❦

Jack the Paperboy swung his feet in the air above the sidewalk. They didn't touch earth because I gathered him by the suspenders with both hands and held him at eyelevel. Toe headed, freckled nose, bad breath, and a flat hat.

"What did you see, kid?"

He pointed across the street. "He came off a bus. From over there. I was huddled down eating an apple when I saw him. He pulled the guy off of them steps and wrestled something outta his hands."

"What?"

"I dunno. He tossed it up there." He pointed at the awning over the apartment entrance. "It didn't come back down. Then he put something in his coat pocket, a large brown envelope I think."

Satisfied, I lowered the squirming imp till both his shoes landed hard.

"That's worth a nickel, I guess."

"You haven't got a nickel!" He pulled out a tally book from his pants and pencil nub from behind his ear. "Let me see here. Caruso, Conner, Cooper. Yeah, Cooper. Here it is. You're shy about a month."

He had me there. I fished a couple of singles out of my wallet and stuffed them in his shirt pocket. "I want a receipt, kid."

"You'll get it the day I own the paper." With this, he kicked me in the shin, dropped the morning Post at my feet, and ran.

Spunky cuss. Jack probably would own the whole rag one day. I made a mental note to expect my receipt on his twenty-first birthday.

***

While waiting for Tumbles to find a ladder, I took a quick perusal of the doings in Denver and a certain article brought my attention to an update on the City and County Office announcing the choice of the Chester Country Club as the next big thing. Continued on the back page more about meeting a deadline and securing sought after contracts.

Tumbles placed the ladder against the wall and once I'd climbed high enough to see, and agitated some pigeons, I got a gander at what the thug in my room this morning probably thought I'd already found. O'Dell's valise and inside the handwritten note from the City Planning Office door. All of it right above my head from day one. "Need a penmanship sample from Miss P. Baxter," I said to Tumble's quizzical stare below the soles of my shoes. "Think I'll deliver her some flowers."

❦

Upon further reflection, I decided delivering the flowers myself wouldn't work. She'd already seen me. So, the task fell to Baylee with instructions to leave the office door open where I could see the transaction take place.

The little chauffeur, sans uniform and now dressed as a deliveryman, played his part to the limit, speaking a little louder than necessary.

With a dozen red stem roses wrapped in white pa-
per he glanced at a little card and asked the secretary, "You Phyllis Baxter?"

She pointed at the placard with her nail file.
He dropped the flowers on the desk and handed her a receipt pad. "Sign here."

Without even a glance at the roses, she stood and did as asked.

"Hey," Baylee said with a big grin. "You're quite a looker." He pointed to the Bullet camera hanging from a strap around his neck. "Got this new yesterday. Mind if I take your picture. I need the practice."

"Sure, little man. Why not?" Teasingly, she struck a pose. "How's this?"

"Great!" He peered into the viewfinder and snapped.

As she arranged into another starlet pose, I heard Harmon, the City Planner, storm out of his office. "What is going on here?"

Baylee turned on his heels and aimed the camera at the man. "Say 'cheese'."

"What?" The tall, heavy man blustered and from my vantage point I saw maps scatter on the floor as he must have knocked the literature rack off the wall.

"Get out of here!"

"Yes, sir. Right away." Baylee turned to the secretary and held out his palm.

She shrugged and fished a nickel out of her little can.

Baylee flipped it in the air. "Thanks, lady!"

Out of the corner of my eye, I caught sight of Chester, the wiry land developer approaching. He didn't give Baylee a second glance as he skirted him through the door and eyed Harmon and the secretary as they grabbed maps from the floor.

"What gives?" he asked.

Harmon blustered and pointed at Baylee. "Idiot delivery boy."

My little *compadre* turned, stood his ground, and stuck his tongue out at them. The shock on their collective faces were priceless and captured forever as Baylee snapped a photo of the trio for posterity.

❦

We compared the secretary's signature to the handwritten note from the door. No match.

"Well, it was a good try anyway," Baylee offered.

"Get those pictures developed." I told him.

"Sure thing. Need a lift anywhere?"

"No, Baylee Boy. Think I'm going to ride the bus around town for a while and see what adds up."

❦

When I boarded the #23 at the corner of 16th & Arapahoe, the stocky bus driver came across as tired and grouchy. His rolled up shirt sleeves exposed an Army tattoo on his forearm and his noggin sported a motor pool flat top. His age appeared to be about right for a recent discharge. The name patch on his coat read 'McCay' so I took a shot. "Long shift, Mac?"

Apparently not used to people talking to him, it took a moment for an answer. "Pulled my usual. Midnight to noon. Evenin' guy's wife havin' a baby. Double shift."

"Sorry to hear it."

He nodded his thanks and motioned me to sit.

I did and settled in on the left side of the bus, half-way back, for a tour of Denver, hoping he didn't nod off somewhere during our excursion. The ride proved enlightening as it bounced along. I saw everything from the Daniels and Fisher Tower, past the Paramount Theater, a lot of the city's retail hub, some cafeterias, and out to Sloan's Lake. For the first time I really got a good look at the Rockies. To date I'd never ventured toward them any closer than the foothills and I wondered if Mary Smith might like to take a trip now as I had access to a chauffeur and a car I didn't have to drive myself.

Several passengers shuffled on and off along the way. A couple of old hens toddled on and perched themselves across the right front bench. At Mann Jr. High School a young lady with blond curls boarded.

Mac made eye contact with her and scowled.

She looked to be the beautician type and after a teasing pout, sat in the seat two rows ahead of me.

Out near where we doubled back at E. 48th a dapper man bounded up the steps and dropped onto the seat next to her. He flirted until she started to giggle.

The big bus screeched to a halt and like a bull, Mac the driver came loose from his spot and startled the two old hens out of their wrinkled skin.

"Hey, bub!" The shirt sleeves slid an inch higher.

"Mind yer own business, pal!" The wolf's voice went incrementally falsetto.

With a, "This *is* my business," Dapper Man, sailed out the door and into the ditch with all the grace of a wounded duck.

The giggler sat ridged, eyes forward, nose in the air.

One of the hens clucked. "Serves him right."

The other cackled back. "Why, the nerve! And in public!"

Mac the driver slapped imaginary dust off his pants and returned to his seat. His glare into the rear-view mirror above his head shamed the giggler to lower her chin.

I smiled and nodded toward the door to indicate my approval of Dapper Man's banishment.

A rev of the motor and Mac slid the transmission into gear without so much as a grind, then floored the peddle.

The probable beautician stoically debussed with the hens a stop before I exited at 16th and Arapahoe, the vehicle having never passed my apartment. The scene of O'Dell's demise and my attack.

Now, how did Vyne suggest I view this?

Take it apart and examine it from all angles.

A good pointer maybe.

Wasn't working for me.

I'm a big picture guy and the big picture contained some scenery that didn't belong.

※✦❧

In what I now refer to as the 'game' room, Vyne and I sat and discussed each of the murder scenes and the entire bus ride in detail.

At last he leaned back in his creaky chair and stared at me.

"What?"

"You've come to a conclusion, haven't you?"

The old bean was sharp, I'll give points there. "I'm at ninety-five percent."

"What will it take to close the final five?"

I rubbed my chin and stood to walk the room. "I'm certain as to the 'why'. Almost certain as to 'how' it's tied in to the other killings."

"Careful here, Mr. Cooper. It's the 'who'." He joined me next to the table with the Oriental game. "The 'who' is a sticking point."

"Exactly." I shrugged. "It's the most important one."

"Perhaps. Reason it out loud. One point at a time."

For the next ten minutes I did precisely that. In the end I narrowed it to two suspects where all the pieces fit.

Vyne stood facing me and smiled.

"But, which one?"

"What if we invited them all to a party?" he asked.

"Huh? A party? All?"

"Yes, we'll throw a great gathering with pomp and circumstance." He held his arms out as if taking in the whole castle. "We'll even invite young Jack, the paperboy. Fill their bellies and put them all at ease. When the time is ripe, we'll lay our case before the lot and see who flinches first."

"So, you haven't identified who it is either?"

"Mr. Cooper, I've followed your logic and it is sound. It will be one or the other of the two you suspect and before the night is over," he said with a wink, "you'll know who murdered my nephew."

TWELVE

The guests arrived in waves, appropriate I guess since the streets were flooding from rainfall which had settled in for a long stay over the city.

Rick stoically accepted wet overcoats, umbrellas, and men's hats at the front door while Silent Stewart escorted our visitors to what I'd call the 'grand' room. Here, Baylee maneuvered around Davenports, wingbacks, and club chairs with a cart of teapots, teacups, and fresh baked cookies. He had instructions to keep his head low around the City Planning gang.

It all felt strangely upscale and homey at the same time. And while I don't comprehend the difference between Mozart and Monet, I did put the platter on the old Victrola and cranked it to life myself, so I can attest to the former as Symphony No. 40 subtly tickled our ears for the evening.

Isn't it amazing how a group of people who aren't acquainted with each other can still manage to meander into groups by perceived social class? Of course, it didn't seem strange for Harmon and his wife, Chester and his wife, and Miss Phyllis Baxter to flock to the cabinet of curios on the left of the room. It also didn't seem strange for Tumbles, Mrs. Hidalgo (sans baby Hidalgo), and Prunella Parks to do the opposite and assemble behind a settee to my right.

We'd invited the #23 bus driver, as a possible someone who had put eyeballs on the killer. Detective Raft, in his usual layers, also got an invitation and ambled near McCay by the warm fireplace on the distant side of the room. Griz Asher, in a gray suit too short in the cuffs, leaned against a doorframe at one of the three exits and tried to look like a civilian. Officer Boggs, in similar plain clothes, did the same near the kitchen entry. Since the gang from my apartment building had all been in proximity of the local force, I moseyed over and politely asked them not to give the boys in blue away. "Don't spill the beans. It's a friendly little party," I told them.

"Jonas, who are all these *other* people?" asked Tumbles. "We do not know any of them."

I turned my back on the bunch from the City and County Building and lowered my voice even more. "Guy in the bowtie. Name's Chester. Double breasted suit is Harmon. They pay *his* salary with *your* taxes. The dame in the pink jacket dress is Harmon's secretary. The stout one in the lavender print is his wife. Little lady in the swagger coat is Chester's missus."

"I wonder where she found that turban?" whispered Prunella Parks as she touched her own pedaline straw hat. "Must have set her back at least four dollars."

"The secretary?"

"Of course the secretary," she whispered. "If she can even type. And the little veil over her eyes, don't you think it's a bit much, Mrs. Hidalgo?"

"Scandalous."

"See."

Lightning flashed through the two street windows on opposite sides of the fireplace.

"Clearly," I agreed.

"Who's the other lady? The young brunette in the dotted frock?"

I'd noticed her when she came in, but assumed Vyne invited her. "Something familiar about the dame, but I haven't a clue. Maybe she came with the cops."

The bus driver I didn't elaborate on as he was obvious in his uniform. He looked haggard, past his bedtime, and completely out of place.

I excused myself and journeyed over to the fireplace. My position blocked his line of sight and he inched to the left. I turned to line out his gaze. He was studying the brunette. Maybe not so tired after all.

"What's the story here? I get a visit from that funny talking guy with an invite to this place. I don't..." Mac broke eye contact with the dotted frock. "Hey, haven't..." He let out a huge yawn. "Haven't I seen you before?"

"Recently." I nodded. "You've got a good eye for faces."

"Yeah. Helps..." He yawned some more air out of the room. "Helps with the tips when you remember folks."

"I can imagine." I pulled a photo from my coat pocket and was going to show it to him when, just as the music on the Victrola stopped, our host for the evening entered the room. "Oh, brother. Get a load of this."

Arcadia Vyne was dressed to the nines in top hat with tails and he tapped a cane on the leg of a glass table in front of the fireplace. "Welcome, welcome! Everyone! I hope you have all enjoyed the assortment of teas this evening. Feel free to try something new." He motioned toward Baylee and the cart. "For your amusement we have *Lapsong Souchong* from the Fujian province. You'll discover a strong smoky flavor. Then, there's the aromatic *Nilgiri* from Tamil Nadu and *Sun Moon Lake* from Taiwan with a hint of honey, cinnamon, and peppermint."

His audience looked absolutely clueless.

"*Earl Grey* and *Lady Earl Grey* are also here tonight and I must say from the sound of the weather outside, those two are most appropriate. And lastly, my own house tea, *Vyne Extraordinaire!*" As he spoke he moved to the center of the room to where a small pedestal table stood.

Did I forget to mention Caffeine the cat had been sleeping there the whole time? The feline paid no notice to the party or the thunder or the lightning.

"Obviously, you all don't know each other. I like to invite an eclectic mix of the population to my get-togethers. Makes for interesting conversation, don't you think?"

Surely he'd noticed everyone standing in their little coveys. Hadn't he?

With white gloved hand, Vyne stroked the back of

the cat from head to tail. It accepted the affection by arching its back and returning a wide yawn. "Now, shall we eat first?" he asked as he surveyed each face in the room. "Or, reveal a killer?"

Food became the second order of business as all went silent enough for the patter of rain on the lace covered windows to punctuate the moment.

"I thought as much." Vyne removed his top hat and handed it to Rick. "Does anyone here like to play games?"

Harmon pulled a handkerchief from the breast pocket of his coat and dabbed sweat from his forehead. "You had us going for a minute there, old man."

Vyne's eyebrows arched. "How so, Mr. Harmon?"

"Well, a parlor game--"

Thunder rattled the art on the wall.

"The very best kind of parlor game!" Vyne smiled and removed his gloves. These he placed in the top hat in Rick's hand. "With consequences!"

The lights suddenly went out and ladies screamed.

When illumination returned a second or two later I stifled a laugh as I noticed Silent Stewart with his hand on the switch.

Vyne was going all out for effect and his theatrics worked as everyone's nerves advanced to the edge of their respective fears.

"I say!" Chester adjusted his bow tie. "What is this? Some kind of hullabaloo?"

Baylee moved chairs to the center of the room and motioned for everyone to take a seat.

With a little teacup and saucer in his big mitt, McCay made one sorry picture of a bus driver in need of a friend.

Feeling bad for him, I decided on a trip to the kitchen to fetch us both a cup of coffee.

Here I found a bustle of activity with a bevy of female caterers making the place a home away from home. One of the older cooks was mothering young Jack at the table with a glass of milk and his own plate of fresh baked cookies.

Two mugs in hand, I reentered the grand room and found the bus driver still at the fireplace leaning on the mantle where he'd abandoned his tea. "Here, you look like you can use this."

"Thanks." He swigged the coffee without hesitation.

"Everyone," encouraged Vyne, "gather in close."

Begrudgingly all did except for Griz Asher, Officer Boggs, myself, and the staff. Even Raft settled in between Prunella Parks and Mrs. Hidalgo on the deep padding of one of the carved wood couches.

Vyne selected a large, high backed chair in between the two factions. Settled, he turned to Prunella Parks and asked, "Did you bring it?"

Somewhat embarrassed she nodded to Rick, who handed her a large canvas bag. From it she extracted a sketchpad and pencil.

Chester cleared his throat. "Again, I ask. What is this?"

"Oh, this dreadful thunder." Chester's dainty wife pulled a handkerchief from the pocket of her husband's coat and fanned herself. "It's more than I can stand."

"Patience Mr. & Mrs. Chester. Patience." Vyne again turned his attention to the artist. "I've asked Miss Parks to do a portrait of someone. She will work while we talk. When she is finished, she will reveal it to us and you can all try to guess who it is."

Lightning flashed and the City and Planning Office's secretary jumped in her seat.

"It's okay, Miss Baxter," consoled her boss to his wife's obvious consternation.

Griz Asher bumped a lamp and while he didn't break it, he did shatter the awkward silence.

"I've seen Miss Parks' drawings," I said to pull attention back into the circle. "She's pretty good. It won't be hard to figure it out."

Prunella Parks stood, thanked me with a slight curtsey, and started her circumnavigation of the room, careful at all times to keep her lines and shading close to her person and out of sight of the others.

Arcadia Vyne nodded at me. "Mr. Cooper, are you prepared to lay out the evidence?"

"I am." With this, I moved to the center of the rug and scratched Caffeine under the chin.

"Hey, buster! You were in our office," pointed out Phyllis Baxter. "And that little guy who's been pushin' that cart around was there too!"

Harmon and Chester glanced at each other.

"Correct. The trail went right past your desk."

"What trail?" asked Mrs. Chester.

"You are all aware of the several murders which have taken place in our fair city in the past week or so. Five private investigators. Five ways of doing them in. Tobias Watkins. Stabbed in the neck on the sidewalk in front of the opera house at 16th & Curtis."

Mrs. Harmon spilled her tea on her husband and Rick moved in with a cloth.

"Rio Richards, poisoned cup of coffee in the café at Union Station." I waited for more spillage, but no one did. "Jake Caine. Seventh story brick to the head near the Kittredge. Jerry O'Dell. Lead to the throat on 17th between Stout and California. And the last one being, far as I can tell, Pinky Bronson. Filled his lungs with a good portion of Sloan's Lake out on 23rd."

Harmon fanned his wife who had now swooned. "I must protest! This talk is ghastly!"

Rick appeared with a glass of water and put it in the tall man's paw.

Tumbles squirmed. "Jonas, what has this to do with all of us? Mr. O'Dell, I can see. The awful business in front of my apartment house. But, the others?"

I glanced at Prunella Parks and she tilted the sketch enough to show it about half complete. "The others, Tumbles. All murdered by someone in this room."

"What?" Mrs. Hidalgo appealed to Raft for an answer. Mute to this point in the evening, he did a good job of appearing as confused as she was and shrugged.

The photo I wanted to show the bus driver earlier had gone back in my pocket when Vyne made his entrance. I retrieved it and placed it in front of the attractive lady wearing the dotted frock. "Recognize anyone in this photo?"

She cleared her throat, placed a finger to her chin, and leaned in for a look. "Not before--"

"Good enough!"

The bus driver shuffled his feet and his chair protested under his weight, so I crossed the rug to him next. "Mac, you ever see anyone in this photo at one of your bus stops?"

He huffed a bit of anger and I chalked it up to the lateness of the hour. "Yeah. I seen this one." He put a thumb on a face in the photo."

"More than once?"

"Maybe."

This threw me for a loop. "Maybe?"

"Yeah." His face went red. "I said what I know."

I glanced at Vyne and he smiled.

Things didn't add up. Then they did. I excused myself and went to the kitchen where I found young Jack snoring the varnish off the kitchen table. A cookie next to his nose revived him.

"Whatdayawant, mister?"

I coaxed him further awake and parked the cookie in his hand. "Jack, this is important." I put the photo in his other hand. Have you ever seen anyone in this picture?"

He yawned. "This guy." He took a bite and tapped the face with the other half of the cookie.

"Where?"

"The morning that fella got shot. He's the one what tossed the case in the air."

I scruffed Jack's hair and motioned to one of the

ladies. "Get this kid a baker's dozen and send him home." A gust of wind rattled the windows over the stove and I changed my mind. "Better still, sack him out on the couch in the library. I'll take him home later."

Upon my return to the grand room I found the lot muttering in their little groups. With a quick apology I glanced at our artist for the evening. "Miss Parks, have you finished?"

"All done."

"Will you sign it please?"

"Why, sure." She did so with a flourish of the pencil, tore the paper from the pad, and handed it over to me.

I passed it along to the young lady in the dotted frock, drawing side down. Still didn't have any idea who she was and I figured she'd be the most neutral. "Can you identify who this is a drawing of?"

She peeked and giggled. "I can."

"Is this person in this room?"

"Yes, this person is in this room. The killer?"

Thunder rolled and the rain dashed harder on the windows.

"Miss Parks," I asked. "Did you sketch the person Mr. Vyne asked you to?"

"Sure did, sweetie."

"Very well." I turned to the lady in the dotted frock. "Please show everyone."

Of all the folks in the room, I believe Detective Raft won the prize for the loudest laugh. Followed a close second by Griz Asher in his too small suit over by the door where he guffawed and pointed at the sketch. "She drew Arcadia Vyne!"

Everyone else joined in the frivolity as the tension seemed to evaporate from the room. Even Caffeine waved her tail in a jaunty manner.

I took the drawing from the lady in the chair and walked it over to Asher. "Please, sir (and I found it difficult calling him 'sir' even though he was undercover) will you read the name of the artist?"

Asher's face went as white as his moniker.

"Signed by..."

"P. Baxter?"

"What?" This from the secretary. "What's the deal? *My* name is Phyllis Baxter. I thought you said her name is Parks. What's she doin' signin' *my* name on that thing?"

I again retrieved the sketch and handed it over to the secretary. "Her name *is* Parks. Miss Parks is an advertising artist. I'd seen how she'd signed her work when I interviewed her in her apartment studio. 'P. Baxter'. And why do you do this, Miss Parks?"

She returned to her seat. "It's a man's world in New York. In the business they recognize me as... Paul Baxter."

"And you are listed in the phone directory as Paul Baxter?"

"I had it put in as P. Baxter. Same as the signature."

I stepped back to see everyone in the room. "Jerry O'Dell found a note on the door of the City Planning Office the Saturday morning he died. He'd been instructed by the firm of Henrich, Montgomery, and Clay to deliver some drawings of a land development project on the very morning of the deadline. The office was supposed to be open and he was to deliver the material to a P. Baxter, the secretary at the City Planning Office. But someone forged a note with her name on it to go to the apartment of another P. Baxter on 17th Street. This note was stuck on a nail in the door of the office for O'Dell to find. He assumed P. Baxter of this office to be the same P. Baxter who lived in the third floor apartment on 17th. Seems Phyllis Baxter had taken a trip to Red Rocks with her boyfriend, Mr. Harmon. Thus the office was closed--"

The thud came from Mrs. Harmon falling out of her seat and onto the floor. Mr. Harmon was too flustered to accept another glass of water and spilled it on her head. At last he stood as his wife took comfort from the Chesters.

"I protest!" he fumbled.

"Sit, Mr. Harmon. Cuddle with your wife *or* your girlfriend," I ordered. "Makes no difference to us."

I felt bad when Mrs. Harmon swooned again, but what was said, was said. "So, O'Dell complies with orders, hoofs it out to his car, and finds two flat tires. He then walks the several blocks to the front of Tumble's apartment building, steps up to the door, and gets one slug through the throat and another through the ear as payment for following directions."

"He had the package I was supposed to get?" asked Prunella Parks.

"Backup plan in case it actually got delivered. Not needed because the killer put two in O'Dell and drug him off the steps as he wrestled the case from him. The cheap handcuffs broke and poor Jerry hit his head. That's what actually put him in a box. Next, the killer grabs the drawings from the case and tosses same onto the awning, unaware the note from the nail on the door is still in it."

"For what purpose?" This from Mrs. Hidalgo.

"You see, when a parcel of land comes up for development in this city there is a period of time folks can submit their drawings for consideration. In this case two - 'Adams Acres' west of Overland Park and

'The Chester Country Club' southwest of the Platte River and Alameda. In the City Planning Office 'Adams Acres' has a big X slashed across it. The plans for 'Adams Acres' never arrived before the deadline. Isn't this correct, Mr. Chester? So, it officially fell out of the running."

"I don't know what you're referring to."

"You won the city contract by default. That worthless land of yours suddenly became extremely valuable when you killed O'Dell and intercepted the 'Adams Acres' drawings."

"You have no proof."

"*Au contraire.* We have a witness who puts you at the scene." I produced the photo again. "Here we have a nice shot of Miss Phyllis Baxter, Mr. Harmon, and you, Mr. Chester. Taken in the City Planning Office. This very evening our witness pointed to your face in this photo, Mr. Chester, and identified you."

Detective Raft came to life, pulled the lapel of his coat back to reveal his badge, and rested the stem of his pipe on his lower lip. "Good enough for me, Cooper." He stood. "Sergeant Asher, take this man into custody for the murder of the five flatfoots. Obvious from what we've heard tonight he wanted to cover up the murder of O'Dell by doing in the others to obscure the motive." He looked through his thick lenses into Chester's eyes. "You're a sick man. Multiple murders for profit. You're done for, pal."

"But, I only shot O'Dell. I didn't... I didn't..."

Asher had the cuffs on him and pulled the prisoner out of the arms of his shocked wife. "Come on, fella. Tell it to a judge." He motioned to Boggs. "Get this lowlife down to the station."

Rick moved in to gather their teacups.

"But, Sergeant. Don't we get to eat first?"

"Do as I say, Boggs. I'm right behind you."

"Yes, sir." The annoyed copper gave me the stink eye. "Thanks for nothin', Pajamas."

"See?" Rick grinned and whispered, "Nicknames lose their amusement when--"

"Yeah. Yeah." I waved him off. "Go pour some tea."

With Chester out of the picture, his wife sobbed in the arms of the likewise sobbing Mrs. Harmon and together they headed for the exit.

Raft pointed a finger at the trailing City Planner, Harmon. "You're an accessory in crime. You pay a visit to the station too."

During all of this you'll note how Arcadia Vyne has been silent, a mere witness to the proceedings.

As Raft headed to the door he addressed his host. "Vyne, all and all a good night's work for your man

Cooper there. Nabbing the killer of five men."

"The evening is just getting started, Detective." Vyne smiled as he accepted a fresh cup of tea from Rick. "Mr. Chester did indeed kill my nephew and I'm indebted for Mr. Cooper in discovering so. However..."

"What?" Raft grabbed Harmon by the arm. "You saying *this* guy killed the other four?"

"No, he may have been in the know about my nephew, but he did not kill anyone."

"But, Chester... I saw the bus driver over here point the guy out in the photo."

"Oh, he pointed out someone all right." I nodded to McCay. "But, it wasn't either one of those two. Was it, Mac?"

"No. It was the dame. The secretary. I'd seen her before at one of my stops."

This is why things didn't tally for me before and I had to go get Jack to point out Chester. What was Vyne up to?

"Vyne, what are you up to?" asked Raft.

Miss Baxter, the secretary, looked positively shell shocked.

"I'm famished. Is anyone else hungry?" Vyne motioned to Baylee. "Tell the ladies to serve in the dining room. Six less settings. And, Miss Baxter, I know you didn't kill anyone either."

"So, who did?" Raft kicked a chair. "Vyne! Who put those other four guys in the cemetery?"

I have to admit, I wondered myself.

"Shall we retire to the dining room? Everyone?"

❦

The dining room held many more windows than the grand room. This amplified the raging storm outside and the candles on the table offered the only light besides what occasionally flashed off the walls.

Each spot had a little paper placard with a name on it. I'm not sure if Raft noticed, but there were none around the rectangle with the names of the Harmons, the Chesters, Griz Asher, or Boggs. There were, however, cards for Vyne at the head, Mac McCay, Mrs. Hidalgo, Prunella Parks, Rick, Detective Raft, myself at the opposing head, our mystery lady in the dotted frock (her placard simply read 'Zelda'), Silent Stewart, George Arnold (aka Tumbles), Baylee, and Phyllis Baxter.

The meal was beyond description and no one enjoyed it except for Vyne, myself, and the staff.

During dessert Vyne handed a note to one of the catering ladies and she brought it to me.

Flirt with Zelda

I raised an eyebrow he couldn't miss way down there.

He nodded ever so slightly.

So, I did as I was instructed and faster than Louis put Schmeling on the canvas found myself in the same situation under the table. Mac McCay came over the top of the fancy dinner settings without spilling the cherry sauce and I never stood a chance to get out of the way. Jealously really stokes a guy's temper and it can pull him apart at the seams. He'd done it before, on the bus.

Why hadn't I recognized her? Different hair. Different dress. Same giggle. The dapper man from E. 48th flirted with her and green-eyed Mac tossed him in a ditch on his ear.

While Raft and Baylee and Rick tried to pull him off of me, he kept yelling. "I knew I'd find out who you were! It had to be one of you investigatin' guys she was foolin' around with!" Now, he held a fork at my throat. "She's my wife! Mine, you hear? I'm gonna kill you!"

"Not today!" I'd endured enough of this nonsense and planted a fist in the middle of his nose. Killed with a fork? Not in *my* obit. A second jab for good measure and from now on he'll twin my friend Pug.

Meanwhile, Zelda McCay sat quietly at the table in her dotted frock and adjusted her brunette wig back over her blond curls. A big smile acknowledged all the attention she'd suddenly garnered. Some dames enjoy playing mind games with the guys.

I took a deep breath and rubbed the near fork-piercing spot on my throat.

Games of all types were played here in the House of Vyne and Zelda certainly won the tournament's runner-up trophy this round.

❦

"I should have considered there was more than one guy involved." I studied the board for my next move. "Chester's too wiry. The thug who jumped me in my apartment had the vigor of somebody young and scrappy. Otherwise I'd have taken him."

"Detective Raft tells me the developer confessed the name of the person he hired to attack you." Arcadia Vyne surveyed his troops on the square battlefield as well. "A mere boy."

"He'd boxed a few rounds."

"When they went to arrest him..."

"Let me guess. Skipped town. Most likely on a freight train. Figures."

"Jonas, I'm impressed. You discovered the one key stop across the street from the steps of your apartment," Vyne moved a pawn while Caffeine purred in his lap, "was not on McCay's morning bus route."

The bishop moved under my touch. I perceived a twitch in my opponent's smile and pulled the piece back. "So much for things adding up. You suspected as much before I ever boarded that bus. Didn't you, Professor? When we were looking at the map. But, you couldn't cement it in place for positive until I got punched by proxy."

"By proxy?"

"Sure. You tossed your fundamentals out the door and played a hunch. And *that* doesn't sit well in your craw."

"I hired you to find my nephew's killer. You did and I am grateful." He grinned. "The fundamentals required me to use my intuition to explain the other murders."

"Intuition, hunch, gut feeling, guess... Whatever the case, Professor, it bugged you to have to resort to my way. So much so, you punched me with that bus driver's fist." I scanned the board for moves with my eye that wasn't black.

"You have such an imagination, Mr. Cooper."

Arcadia Vyne
will Return
in

The
Day
Nobody
Died

by

Ira Amos

Look
for These Exciting
FICTION TITLES
from
James Kay Publishing

All In Color For A Time
by Michael Vance

The Thief of Two Worlds
by Michael Vance

Mayan Moon
by Derek Bullard

Twice in a Blue Moon
by Derek Bullard

Moon Ridge
by Derek Bullard

Look
for These Informative
NON-FICTION TITLES
from
James Kay Publishing

The Book of Daniel
"The Most High Rules"
by Lucian Farrar, Jr.

Jeremiah
God's Messenger
to an Antagonistic People
by Bob McDoniel

Being the Best Employee You Can Be!
by Derek Bullard

James Kay Publishing
PO Box 470733
Tulsa, Oklahoma 74147

www.jameskaypublishing.com

booktour@jameskaypublishing.com